The Berenstain Bears

"Who are you mocking?
At whom do you sneer and stick out your tongue?"
—Isaiah 57:4

ZONDERKIDZ

The Berenstain Bears® Stand Up to Bullying

Copyright © 2018 by Berenstain Publishing, Inc.
Illustrations © 2018 by Berenstain Publishing, Inc.

This book is also available as a Zondervan ebook.

Requests for information should be addressed to:

Zonderkidz, 3900 Sparks Dr. SE, Grand Rapids, Michigan 49546

ISBN 978-0-310-76445-8

Design: Cindy Davis

Printed in the United States of America

18 19 20 21 /CWM/ 23 22 21 20 19 18 17 16 15 14 13 12 11 10 9 8 7 6 5 4 3 2

By Mike Berenstain
Based on the characters created by
Stan & Jan Berenstain

Everyone in Bear Country knew Too-Tall Grizzly and his gang were bullies—a teasing-taunting, pushing-shoving, heckling-hassling bunch of bullies. But what everyone did not know was that bullies like them could get bullied themselves. It all came out when Brother, Sister, and Honey Bear paid a visit to Farmer Ben's farm.

The three cubs were on their way to help Mrs. Ben pick apples for her special apple pie. Nearing the farm's orchard, they heard voices—angry voices. Peeking around the trunk of an apple tree, they saw the Too-Tall Gang in the middle of an argument.

"Get up that tree, Skuzz!" Too-Tall yelled to one of the gang. "Throw down some apples to us! That's an order!"

"But, Chief!" whined the cub they called Skuzz. "That tree is really high, and I'm not much of a climber."

"Ha! Ha!" taunted the gang. "Skuzz is scared! Skuzz is a chicken!"

They began to flap their arms and cluck like chickens.

"Bawk! Bawk!" they clucked. "Skuzz is a chicken! Skuzz is a chicken!"

Skuzz was scared. But he didn't want the gang to think he was chicken. So, he gritted his teeth and began to climb.

As Brother, Sister, and Honey watched, Skuzz slowly climbed the tree.
Shakily, he reached for an apple. But he reached too far and slipped.
"Oh, no!" gasped Sister.

Luckily, Skuzz caught a branch under his knees and dangled upside down.

"Help!" he yelled. "HEEEELP!"

But the gang just laughed.

"Now Skuzz is flyin' like a bird!" they cackled and flapped their arms.
"Tweet! Tweet!" they sang. "Skuzz is a birdy!"

"Why, those no-good bullies!"
growled Brother as he began to
march out to put a stop to things.

That's when Mrs. Ben appeared. She had been hiding inside the hollow trunk of an old apple tree and jumped out to grab Too-Tall by the back of the neck.

"Gotcha, you varmints!" she cried. "Lucky I heard you coming into the orchard and hid myself."

"Leggo!" said Too-Tall. "We didn't do nuthin'!"

"What about your friend dangling up there?" asked Mrs. Ben. "You call that 'nuthin'?"

"Oh, don't worry about Skuzz," said Too-Tall. "He has a thick skull. If he falls, it won't hurt him ... *much*!"

"Not as thick as *your* skull, I'll warrant," snorted Mrs. Ben.

"Now, you three young scamps skedaddle up that tree and fetch that poor feller down," ordered Mrs. Ben.

They skedaddled. No one crossed Mrs. Ben when her dander was up. As they helped Skuzz get down, Brother, Sister, and Honey joined Mrs. Ben.

"Why, hello there, cubs!" said Mrs. Ben. "I was expecting you. Did you witness all this commotion?"

"Yes, we did!" said Sister. "I never realized that bullies even bully each other sometimes."

"Anyone can be the victim of bullying," said Mrs. Ben. "And there hangs a tale—just like this young'un hanging from that apple tree. Did you cubs ever hear the story of Joseph and his brothers?"

The cubs shook their heads.
"It's from the Bible," said Mrs. Ben.

Too-Tall rolled his eyes but stopped when Mrs. Ben caught him.

"Long ago, in the Holy Land," began Mrs. Ben, "there lived a man named Jacob ... "

"Now, Jacob had twelve sons," Mrs. Ben went on. "But his favorite was his youngest, Joseph. Jacob gave him a special gift—a coat of many colors. This made the other brothers so jealous they plotted against Joseph. They stole his coat and threw him in a pit!"

"Tsk! Tsk!" said Skuzz. "His own brothers!"

"The brothers decided to sell Joseph into slavery in the land of Egypt," said Mrs. Ben.

"Wow!" said Too-Tall, impressed. "Harsh!"

"Years later," continued Mrs. Ben, "Joseph gained his freedom and met his brothers once again. At first he was very angry with them."

"Well, naturally," said Skuzz.

"But his brothers were very sorry for what they had done so long ago," said Mrs. Ben. "And Joseph forgave them. They all wept and embraced each other."

"That's nice!" said Skuzz.

"Now," said Mrs. Ben, "do you young scalawags want to be like the brothers of Joseph, picking on one of your own and others?"

"No, Ma'am," mumbled the gang, embarrassed.

"Why, your friend here might have been seriously hurt falling out of that tree," exclaimed Mrs. Ben. "Is that what you want?"

"Well, no," admitted Too-Tall. "We wouldn't want Skuzz to get hurt … much!"

"There, now!" said Mrs. Ben. "Lesson learned. Come along with me and have some of my special apple pie."

"Oh, boy!" cheered the cubs.

"And," added Mrs. Ben, "we'll have no more of this confounded bullying! Understood?"

"Yes, Ma'am!" they replied. And they meant it.

No one crossed Mrs. Ben when she was offering her special apple pie.